Five reasons why w̶e̶ you'll love this

Winnie and Wilbur
AT CHINESE NEW YEAR

See Winnie's house transformed into glorious red and gold!

Learn some Chinese words! 新年快乐 (sheen nian kwai luh) means 'Happy New Year'!

There is so much to spot in every picture.

Celebrate with Winnie and Wilbur, Chinese style!

You c... do you kn... ...bur challenge: ...imal it is this year?

Fang Xuhao

Lily

Kevin

Chen Xuanyu

Claire

Grace

Jone

Wendy

Happy

Valentin

Dante

Liany Wenxu

Kevin

Bolly Diamond

Thank you to LIPA Primary School, Liverpool
and to children across China
for helping with the endpapers.

For Helen Mortimer—V.T.

For Jason Tzannes with love—K.P.

OXFORD
UNIVERSITY PRESS

Great Clarendon Street, Oxford OX2 6DP

Oxford University Press is a department of the
University of Oxford. It furthers the University's
objective of excellence in research, scholarship,
and education by publishing worldwide.
Oxford is a registered trade mark of
Oxford University Press in the UK and
n certain other countries

Database right Oxford University Press (maker)

First published in 2020

British Library Cataloguing in Publication Data available

ISBN: 978-0-19-277237-4 (paperback)
978-0-19-277238-1 (paperback and CD)

10 9 8 7 6 5 4 3 2 1

Printed in China

Paper used in the production of this book is a natural, recyclable
product made from wood grown in sustainable forests. The
manufacturing process conforms to the environmental
regulations of the country of origin

www.winnieandwilbur.com

Winnie the Witch sat in her rocking chair and felt very bored.
'I want something exciting to do, Wilbur,' Winnie said.

Wilbur, Winnie's big black cat, was asleep.
Wilbur never felt bored.

Winnie looked at her phone.
'Celebrate Chinese New Year,' it said.
She scrolled down.

Celebrate Chinese New Year:
Food.
Decorations.
New Clothes.
Food.
Dragons.
Family and friends.
Food.
Lions.
Fireworks.
Food.

It sounded wonderful.
Food? Wilbur woke up. Wilbur liked
anything with food.

'That's what we'll do,' Winnie said.
'We'll invite all our friends and
family to a Chinese New Year party.'

Now Winnie didn't feel bored.
She felt excited.
'First we have to clean the house,'
Winnie said.

Winnie and Wilbur jumped onto her
broomstick, and they swept and dusted
and polished until the house
was sparkling clean.

Then Winnie put the broomstick in the cupboard.
'We mustn't sweep during Chinese New Year,
in case we sweep away good luck,' she said.

'Now we need some decorations,' said Winnie.
She found some paper, scissors, glue,
and glitter and made some shiny red lanterns.

They looked good, but not fantastic.
Then Winnie had a very good idea.
She waved her magic wand, shouted,

'Abracadabra!'

. . . and *everything* in
Winnie's house was red and gold.
It looked fantastic.

'Now for the food,' Winnie said.
'I wonder what kind of food you
eat for Chinese New Year?
Dumplings? Spring rolls?
Sticky rice cakes?'

Then Winnie had an excellent idea.
She found a spell to make a
Chinese New Year banquet.
She waved her magic wand, shouted,

'Abracadabra!'

. . . and there was a delicious
Chinese New Year banquet.
It looked delicious.
It smelled delicious.

The guests came crowding in.
They picked up the chopsticks
and ate and ate and ate.
But eating with chopsticks
wasn't easy.
Plop! Splash! Splosh!

快
乐

Winnie had made too much food.
So she put a notice on her front gate.
**CELEBRATE CHINESE NEW YEAR.
FOOD AND FUN.**

More and more people crowded in.
Everybody was having a happy time.

'Now we'll have the big parade,'
Winnie said, 'with costumes!'
She waved her magic wand and shouted,

'Abracadabra!'

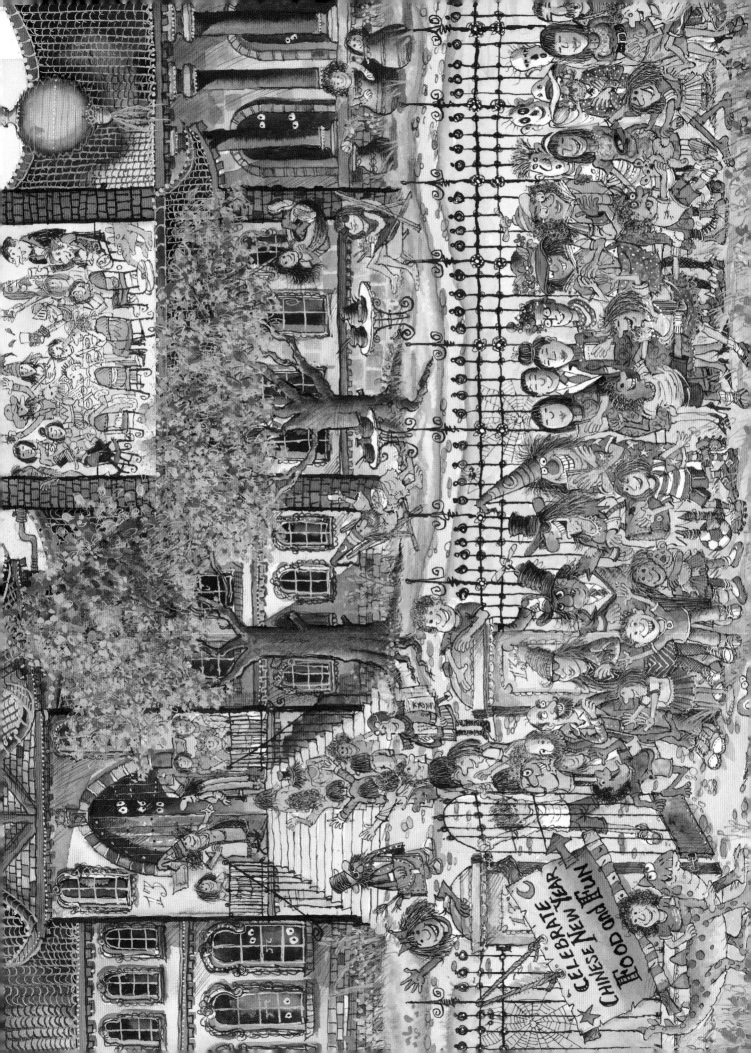

There was a big dragon,
some baby dragons, lions,
and one funny little baby lion.

The big dragon was being paraded
around the garden,
the baby dragons and the lions
danced and pranced . . .

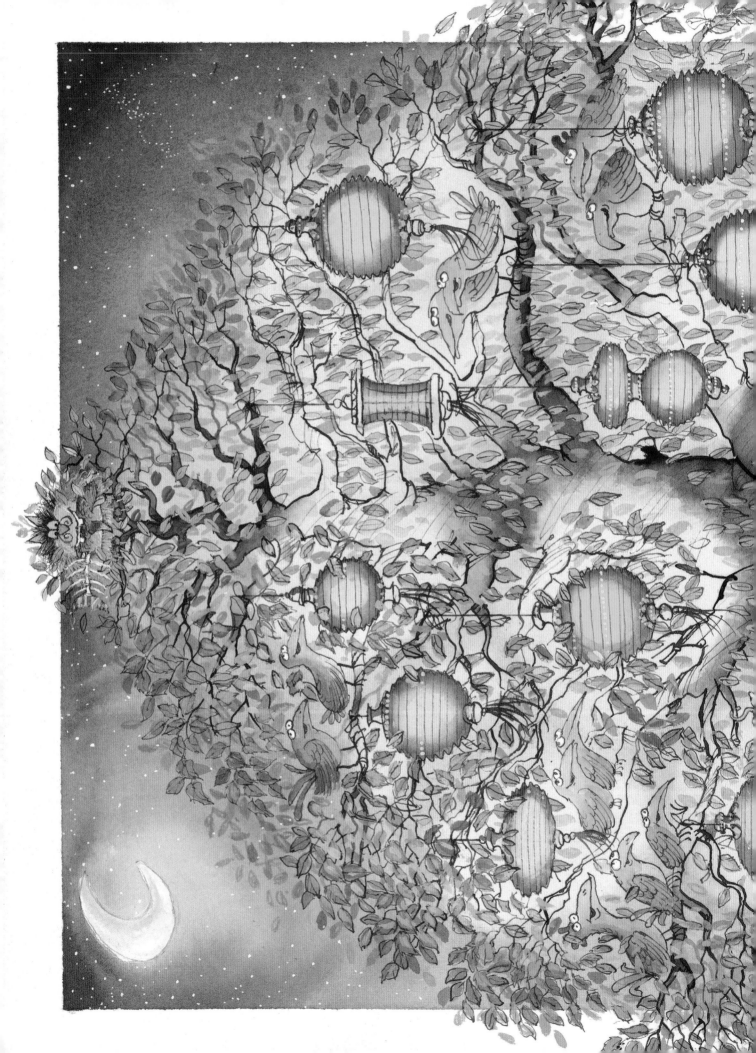

. . . and climbed up to the top of the tallest tree to eat it. It was delicious.
I'll climb down and get another one, thought the baby lion. Nobody will see me.

but the funny little baby lion just wanted to eat.
It took some dumplings and a spring roll. Then it grabbed a big fish from the banquet table . . .

It was time for the fireworks.
'Come and watch the fireworks,
Wilbur,' Winnie said.
'Wilbur? Wilbur?
Where are you, Wilbur?'

Winnie looked everywhere. Her guests helped her look.
He wasn't in the garden. He wasn't in the house.
He wasn't at the top of the tallest tree.

He had disappeared.
Winnie was worried.

The baby lion crept up to
the banquet table.
Nobody was watching.
They were all looking for Wilbur.

It jumped onto the table
and grabbed another big fish.

But Winnie was watching.
'Get down, you greedy little lion,'
shouted Winnie.

Then she looked carefully at the lion.
'**Meow**,' it said.
'Is that you, Wilbur?' asked Winnie.
She waved her magic wand, shouted,

'Abracadabra!'

. . . and there was Wilbur,
purring.

'Oh Wilbur, did my spell turn
you into a greedy little lion?'
Winnie said.
'I'm glad you're a cat again!'

So am I, thought Wilbur,
but that fish was delicious.

WHOOSH! FLASH!
went the fireworks.

'Oooh! Aaah!'
went the guests.

Then there was one enormous flash . . .

. . . red packets fell from the sky
and everybody had a present.

'Happy New Year!' shouted Winnie.
'Happy New Year!' shouted all the guests.
'Purr, purr, purr,' said Wilbur.

Chen Jiexin

Anne

Alice

Shu Yiyang

Sara

Dora

Febe

Tom

Fan Yuchen

Adina

William

Ava

Abel

Kevin Wu

A note for grown-ups

Oxford Owl is a FREE and easy-to-use website packed with support and advice about everything to do with reading.

Informative videos

Hints, tips and fun activities

Top tips from top writers for reading with your child

Help with choosing picture books

For this expert advice and much, much more about how children learn to read and how to keep them reading ...

LOOK
for Oxford Owl
www.oxfordowl.co.uk